ALIEN – BENEATH OUR SKIES

POONAM PACHOURI

Contents

About The Book

Aliens-What Beneath Our Skies is About

Beneath Our Skies is a thrilling and emotional sci-fi novel that delves into themes of identity, survival, and the enduring connections that make us human—even when one of us isn't.

The story follows Lucas Wright, an alien fugitive who has spent decades hiding on Earth, blending into the quiet town of Evergreen. For thirty years, he's maintained a careful façade, keeping his otherworldly nature a secret while living as a reclusive yet unassuming neighbor. But Lucas's peaceful life is shattered when an otherworldly signal alerts his enemies to his location. The Vyrkani Hunters, deadly enforcers from his homeworld, have arrived—and they will stop at nothing to capture or kill him.

As chaos descends on Evergreen, Lucas finds an unexpected ally in Emma Carter, a determined and curious reporter who stumbles onto his secret. Thrust into a dangerous world of intergalactic hunters and hidden technology, Emma must navigate her growing trust in Lucas while questioning everything she thought she knew about the world—and herself.

Together, they race against time to stop the hunters from wreaking havoc on their town and, possibly, the entire planet. Along the way, Lucas and Emma grapple with impossible choices, personal sacrifices, and the hope of a future where secrets no longer divide them. As Lucas faces his pursuers, he also confronts his own guilt and longing for redemption, questioning whether he can truly belong in a world he's spent his life hiding from.

Beneath Our Skies combines high-stakes action with heartfelt human drama, offering readers an immersive story about courage, trust, and the price of keeping—and revealing—our true selves.

CHAPTER ONE

The Stranger in the Shadows

The town of Evergreen was as picturesque as it was predictable. Rows of neatly trimmed hedges lined the streets, and every porch seemed to have a rocking chair, a lazy dog, or a pot of blooming flowers. To an outsider, it looked like a town frozen in time—safe, quiet, and ordinary. But Evergreen was also a place where people noticed everything, and no one noticed that more than Lucas Wright.

Lucas stood by the window of his small, weathered house on Willow Lane, staring out at the neighborhood he'd come to call home. The sun dipped low, painting the sky in hues of orange and purple. Families were settling in for dinner, lights flickering on one by one. The smell of freshly cut grass wafted through the air, mixing with the faint aroma of someone grilling burgers two doors down. It was the kind of scene that made Evergreen feel welcoming. But for Lucas, it was a façade.

For three years, he'd lived here. For three years, he'd pretended to be something he wasn't.

His neighbors thought they knew him—a quiet man with a soft spot for his old dog, Scout, and a knack for fixing computers. They didn't question why he never attended block parties or why he always wore gloves when he worked in his yard. They certainly didn't wonder why his house never seemed to age, no matter how harsh the winters were. To them, Lucas was just... Lucas.

But Lucas wasn't like them. He wasn't like anyone in Evergreen.

Scout let out a low whine, nudging Lucas's leg with her wet nose. The old Labrador was the only creature on Earth who knew his secret—and the only one Lucas trusted. He knelt down, running a hand over her gray-speckled fur.

"Getting late, huh?" he murmured. Scout wagged her tail, her cloudy eyes lifting to meet his.

It was their routine. Every evening, Lucas walked her through the park just as the sun disappeared behind the hills. It was a small risk—being out in public—but it helped him maintain the illusion of normalcy. Besides, Evergreen was safest when people believed he was just like them.

Grabbing Scout's leash, Lucas stepped out into the crisp evening air. The walk was uneventful, as it always was. Kids raced their bikes down the street, laughing and shouting. A man across the park waved, and Lucas waved back. He knew the man's name—Tom Dwyer—and his favorite football team, though they'd never had a real conversation. Lucas made it a point to learn about the people around him. Knowing was safer than being known.

But tonight, something felt... off.

It started with the sound. A low, humming vibration that seemed to come from nowhere and everywhere at once. Lucas froze mid-step, his body instantly alert. Scout stopped, her ears perked up, and let out a soft growl.

Lucas turned his gaze toward the horizon. The sun was gone now, the sky darkening into deep blue, but there was something unusual about the air. It felt heavy, charged, like the seconds before a thunderstorm. The hum grew louder, sending a faint ripple through the ground beneath his feet. It was faint—so faint that a human might have dismissed it as their imagination.

But Lucas wasn't human.

His chest tightened as a chill ran down his spine. He scanned the park, his sharp eyes catching every movement, every detail. Parents herded their children inside, oblivious to the disturbance. The Dwyer kids shouted one last protest before their mother called them in for dinner. Normal life continued around him, blissfully unaware of what Lucas now knew.

This wasn't natural.

The hum wasn't a sound at all. It was a signal—a pulse that resonated with a frequency only Lucas could perceive. He'd felt it once before, years ago, on a planet far from this one. It wasn't a warning. It was a presence.

Something—or someone—was here.

The rest of the walk passed in a haze. Lucas couldn't shake the feeling that he was being watched. He hurried back to the house, locking the door behind him. Scout padded to her bed and flopped down, letting out a tired sigh. Lucas stood in the middle of the living room, his heart pounding.

He knew he should investigate the source of the pulse. But stepping into the open was dangerous. For years, he'd suppressed everything that made him different—his strength, his heightened senses, his connection to the electromagnetic fields that crisscrossed the universe. Using those abilities risked exposure, and exposure meant danger—not just for him, but for everyone in Evergreen.

Instead, Lucas moved to the corner of the room, where the floorboards were slightly uneven. He pried one loose, revealing a hidden compartment. Inside was a spherical device, small enough to fit in his hand, its surface smooth and dark. He hadn't touched it in years, but tonight, he had no choice.

As his fingers brushed the surface, the device came to life, glowing faintly. Lines of alien script scrolled across its surface, pulsing in time with the signal he'd felt earlier. Lucas's heart sank.

The message was simple but chilling: "They are here."

For a long moment, Lucas stared at the glowing device, his mind racing. He'd come to Earth to escape, to hide. He'd chosen this planet because it was overlooked, unimportant—a tiny, unremarkable dot in the vast expanse of the galaxy. But if "they" had found him, it meant they were searching.

It meant his time in Evergreen was running out.

Scout whimpered softly, sensing his unease. Lucas reached down, running a hand over her head, more for his comfort than hers. "It's okay," he whispered, though the words felt hollow. "We'll figure it out."

But deep down, Lucas knew the truth. He couldn't stay hidden forever.

CHAPTER TWO

The Visitor

Lucas barcly slept that night. The message from the device echoed in his mind, a stark reminder of the life he had left behind. As dawn broke, he sat at his kitchen table, staring out the window with a cup of coffee growing cold in his hands. Scout rested at his feet, her head on her paws, occasionally glancing up at him as if to reassure him.

For thirty years, he had avoided situations like this. For thirty years, he'd lived cautiously, blending in and never drawing attention. Yet the signal had been unmistakable. Someone—no, something—was here. And if they had found him, they wouldn't stop until they completed their mission.

A soft knock at the door broke the silence.

Lucas's pulse quickened. He set his coffee mug down, rising from his chair with calculated calm. He moved toward the door but didn't open it right away. Instead, he peered through the peephole, his body tense.

It was Emma Carter.

Lucas relaxed slightly but didn't drop his guard. Emma was Evergreen's most curious soul, the town's unofficial investigator. She had a nose for unusual stories and a habit of showing up at the worst possible times.

Another knock. "Lucas? It's Emma. You in there?" Her voice was chipper but laced with determination.

He sighed, unbolting the door. "Emma. Morning."

She smiled, though her expression quickly turned scrutinizing as her sharp eyes scanned his face. "You look like you've seen a ghost."

"Didn't sleep well," Lucas replied, stepping aside to let her in. "What brings you here?"

Emma didn't wait for an invitation. She walked into the living room, clutching a notepad and her phone, her ever-present tools of the trade. "The blackout last night," she said, getting straight to the point. "You know anything about it?"

Lucas shook his head, keeping his expression neutral. "Not really. Power outages happen."

Emma raised an eyebrow, unconvinced. "This wasn't just a power outage. People's cars wouldn't start. Phones went dead. Even old generators didn't work. That's not normal, Lucas."

He kept his face impassive. "I'm not an electrician, Emma."

She narrowed her eyes, studying him. "You're a tech guy, though. IT wizard. You've got to have some theory."

Lucas felt his jaw tighten. Emma was smart, and more importantly, she was persistent. If he brushed her off too abruptly, she'd only dig deeper. "Maybe a geomagnetic storm?" he suggested, grasping for the most plausible explanation. "They can disrupt electronics."

Emma frowned, jotting something in her notebook. "Maybe. But here's the weird part." She pulled out her phone and swiped to a photo. "Look at this."

Lucas leaned closer. The photo showed a section of the woods near Evergreen Park. Trees had been scorched in a near-perfect circle, the ground beneath them charred and lifeless. His stomach sank.

"This wasn't from lightning," Emma said, her voice quiet now. "And it happened at the same time as the blackout."

Lucas straightened, forcing his expression into one of curiosity. "You sure it's not some kind of prank? Kids messing around?"

Emma shook her head. "No way. I checked it out myself this morning. The area's still warm to the touch, like it's been cooked from the inside."

Lucas rubbed the back of his neck, feigning confusion while his mind raced. The scorched ground could only mean one thing: a landing site. The Vyrkani scouts were here, and they weren't trying to hide it.

"Why are you showing me this?" Lucas asked carefully.

"Because you're the only person in this town who doesn't look at me like I'm crazy," Emma said with a small laugh. "And because... well, you're different, Lucas."

The words hung in the air between them. Lucas froze, his heart pounding in his chest. "Different how?" he asked, his voice measured.

Emma hesitated, then shrugged. "I don't know. You just... don't seem like everyone else. I've always wondered why you're so private, why you don't get involved in town stuff. And now, with this?" She gestured to her phone. "It feels connected."

Lucas forced a chuckle. "You're overthinking it, Emma. I'm just a guy who likes his privacy."

Emma studied him for a moment longer, then sighed. "Maybe you're right. But something's happening, Lucas. And I don't think it's over."

She tucked her phone back into her pocket and turned to leave. At the door, she paused. "If you see or hear anything strange, you'll let me know, right?"

"Of course," Lucas replied, his voice steady.

Emma nodded, then stepped out into the morning light. Lucas watched her go, his mind a whirlwind of thoughts. He'd managed to deflect her suspicions for now, but he knew Emma wouldn't let this go. And worse, the Vyrkani scouts were closer than he'd thought.

That night, Lucas ventured into the woods. He moved silently, his heightened senses scanning the area for signs of activity. The charred clearing Emma had shown him in the photo was easy to find, its edges still smoldering faintly. The air smelled of burnt ozone, a telltale sign of Vyrkani energy fields.

Kneeling, Lucas placed a hand on the ground. A faint vibration hummed beneath his fingertips, almost like a heartbeat. The scouts had left a trail, one that only someone like him could follow.

Lucas straightened, his jaw set. He'd spent decades hiding, avoiding conflict, and suppressing his true nature. But now, the danger was too close. He couldn't sit idly by while Evergreen—and Emma—became collateral damage.

The hunters had come for him. It was time to stop running.

CHAPTER THREE

The Hunter's Mark

The forest was alive with whispers of the past. Lucas moved carefully, his boots crunching on the underbrush, his senses tuned to every shift in the air. The charred ground beneath his feet pulsed faintly, a lingering trace of the Vyrkani's energy. They had left a mark here—one that was both a message and a warning.

Scout had wanted to follow him, as she always did, but this time Lucas left her behind. This was no ordinary walk, and he didn't want her anywhere near what he might find. The Vyrkani were ruthless, and he couldn't afford distractions.

As he reached the edge of the scorched circle, he crouched, his fingers brushing the blackened soil. He closed his eyes, focusing, letting his true self slip past the fragile boundaries of his human guise. Beneath the surface, he was a creature of energy, his senses far sharper than any human's.

He could feel the electromagnetic resonance of the landing site, the faint ripples in the air that told him where they had gone. The hunters had been here only hours ago, and their trail led deeper into the woods.

Lucas exhaled slowly, standing. His muscles tensed, his instincts urging him to run—either toward the danger or away from it, he wasn't sure. For thirty years, he had avoided confrontation, choosing anonymity over heroism. But now, the fight had come to him. The hunters weren't here by coincidence. They had come for him.

And they wouldn't stop until he was dead.

The path they'd taken was subtle but unmistakable. Broken branches, faint scorch marks on tree trunks, the faint hum of energy in the air. Lucas followed it deeper into the forest, his mind racing. The Vyrkani weren't just scouts—they were predators. Efficient, silent, deadly. They wouldn't have landed here without a plan, and that meant he had very little time to act.

As the trail curved toward a rocky outcrop, Lucas paused. The air was thicker here, heavier. He could feel the subtle vibrations of a cloaked energy field nearby. They were close.

He reached into his pocket, pulling out the small spherical device he had hidden for decades. The interface flickered to life, casting a faint blue glow against the dark forest. Lines of alien script scrolled across its surface as it synchronized with the energy field around him.

There it was—a faint shimmer in the air, almost invisible to the naked eye. Lucas pressed a button on the device, and the shimmer sharpened into a translucent barrier. Beyond it, he could see two figures, their silhouettes tall and angular, their movements deliberate and calculated.

Vyrkani.

Lucas clenched his fists, his human façade rippling faintly as his true form fought to surface. He forced himself to stay calm. Charging in headfirst would be suicide. He needed a plan.

The two hunters stood near a small clearing, their voices low and guttural. Lucas couldn't hear their words, but he didn't need to. He knew their mission: to find him, eliminate him, and retrieve any technology he had stolen when he fled Vyrkos. They wouldn't care about the humans in Evergreen—they were collateral damage at best, irrelevant at worst.

Lucas's mind raced. He could disable their cloaking device and draw them into the open, but that would risk exposing himself to the entire town. He could attack now, but without the element of surprise, the odds were against him.

And then he heard it—a soft rustling in the underbrush behind him. Lucas froze, his senses going into overdrive. The hunters hadn't noticed yet, but whatever was behind him wasn't part of the forest.

Slowly, he turned.

"Lucas?"

The whisper was barely audible, but it was enough to make his stomach drop.

Emma stood a few feet away, her flashlight clutched tightly in her hand. Her wide eyes flicked between Lucas and the faint shimmer of the energy barrier in front of him.

"What the hell is this?" she whispered, her voice trembling.

Lucas's mind went blank. He'd been so focused on the hunters that he hadn't sensed her approach. How much had she seen? How much did she know?

"Emma," he said softly, stepping toward her. "You need to leave. Now."

But Emma didn't move. Her gaze was locked on the shimmering field, the vague outlines of the hunters just visible beyond it. "Lucas, what is that? What are they?"

The hunters must have heard her, because their movements stilled. One of them turned, its glowing eyes piercing through the barrier as it scanned the forest.

Lucas grabbed Emma's arm, pulling her down behind a fallen log. "You shouldn't be here," he hissed, keeping his voice low.

Emma yanked her arm free, her expression a mixture of fear and defiance. "And you shouldn't be sneaking around in the middle of the night, staring at... whatever this is!"

Lucas didn't have time to argue. The hunters were moving now, their energy field flickering as they prepared to deactivate it.

"Listen to me," he said, his voice urgent. "You need to go back to town and forget you saw any of this. Do you understand? If you stay here, you'll get hurt."

Emma shook her head, her hands trembling. "Not until you tell me what's going on. Who are they? And who are you?"

The energy field disappeared with a faint crackle, and the hunters stepped into the clearing. Their tall, elongated forms were cloaked in dark armor, their glowing eyes scanning the area. One of them raised a device, emitting a low pulse that made the air vibrate.

"They're searching for me," Lucas said, his voice barely above a whisper. "And if they find us, they'll kill us both."

The hunters moved with eerie precision, their steps silent as they approached. Lucas's mind raced. He couldn't reveal himself to Emma, but he couldn't let the hunters reach her either.

"Stay down," he ordered, rising to his feet.

"Lucas, what are you—"

Before she could finish, Lucas stepped into the clearing, his body tense. The hunters froze, their glowing eyes locking onto him.

"Zarneth," one of them said, its voice a guttural growl. "You've been difficult to find."

Lucas said nothing, his human form flickering faintly as he prepared himself. He could feel Emma's gaze on him, her confusion and fear palpable.

"You don't belong here," the hunter continued, its tone cold. "Come quietly, and we'll make this quick."

Lucas's lips curved into a grim smile. "I'm not going anywhere."

And with that, the forest erupted into chaos.

CHAPTER FOUR

Unveiled

The forest became a battlefield.

Lucas lunged forward, his human façade rippling away as he embraced the energy coursing through his alien body. His form shimmered with light, his skin glowing faintly as his limbs elongated and his posture straightened. His gold-flecked eyes burned brightly, locking onto the hunters with an intensity that made them pause for a split second.

That pause was all he needed.

Lucas thrust his arm out, and a pulse of kinetic energy surged from his palm. The force slammed into the nearest hunter, sending it crashing into a tree. The second hunter wasted no time, raising a device that emitted a sharp, high-pitched whine. Lucas barely dodged the beam that shot from it, rolling to the side as the ground where he had been standing exploded in a burst of heat and light.

"Emma, run!" he shouted, his voice echoing with an otherworldly resonance.

But Emma didn't move. She crouched behind the log, her eyes wide as she watched Lucas in his true form, glowing and fierce, facing off against beings that were equally terrifying. It was impossible, yet here it was, playing out in front of her like some surreal nightmare.

The hunter that had been thrown into the tree recovered quickly, rising with mechanical precision. It moved to flank Lucas, its tall, angular frame emitting faint whirs and clicks as it readied another attack. Lucas spun, a flick of his wrist sending a wave of energy toward it. The hunter absorbed the blow, its armor shimmering as it dissipated the impact.

Lucas gritted his teeth. These weren't ordinary scouts. They were enforcers—elite hunters trained for combat. And they were prepared.

The second hunter advanced, its movements fluid and deliberate. It spoke in the guttural language of their homeworld, its voice filled with disdain. "You've lived among these primitives for too long, Zarneth. You've grown soft."

Lucas didn't respond. He focused on his surroundings, using the forest to his advantage. He ducked behind a tree, dodging another blast from the hunter's weapon, and countered with a surge of energy that splintered the tree into shards. The fragments flew toward the hunter, forcing it to shield itself.

But as Lucas fought, he could feel his strength waning. Maintaining his human form for so long had taken a toll on him, and he hadn't used his abilities in decades. The enforcers were relentless, their attacks calculated and precise. He couldn't keep this up forever.

"Lucas!" Emma's voice rang out, sharp and terrified.

He turned just in time to see one of the hunters advancing toward her. She had broken cover, her flashlight trembling in her hand as she backed away. The hunter raised its weapon, and Lucas's chest tightened.

"No!" he shouted, the word carrying an explosive force.

In an instant, Lucas was in front of her, his body a shield. The hunter fired, and Lucas absorbed the blast, the energy rippling through his glowing frame. The pain was sharp and searing, but he didn't flinch. He raised his hand and released a wave of energy so powerful it sent the hunter flying backward, crashing into the ground with a metallic thud.

Emma stared at him, her mouth open in shock. "What are you?"

Lucas turned to her, his glowing eyes softening. "I'll explain later. But right now, you need to leave."

"But—"

"Go!" he barked, his voice more forceful than he intended.

For once, Emma didn't argue. She turned and ran, disappearing into the shadows of the forest. Lucas exhaled, relieved that she was out of immediate danger. But the battle wasn't over.

The hunters regrouped, their movements synchronized. One of them raised a small, spherical device, its surface glowing faintly. Lucas recognized it immediately—a containment field generator. If they activated it, they would trap him, rendering his abilities useless.

He couldn't let that happen.

Summoning every ounce of his remaining strength, Lucas charged. He moved faster than human eyes could follow, his body a blur of light and motion. He reached the hunter holding the device and struck with precision, knocking it from its grasp. The device tumbled to the ground, emitting a high-pitched whine before deactivating.

But the distraction cost him. The second hunter struck from behind, a blow landing squarely on Lucas's back. Pain exploded through him as he hit the ground, his vision blurring for a moment. The hunter loomed over him, raising its weapon for a finishing blow.

Lucas clenched his fists, drawing energy from the very air around him. With a shout, he released it in a powerful wave, knocking both hunters off their feet. The forest lit up like a flash of lightning, and for a moment, everything was still.

When the light faded, the hunters were gone.

Lucas staggered to his feet, his breathing ragged. He scanned the clearing, his heightened senses searching for any trace of the enforcers. But they had retreated, likely regrouping for another attack. He couldn't relax—not yet. They would return, stronger and more determined than before.

As the adrenaline began to fade, Lucas felt the weight of the battle settle over him. His injuries throbbed, his energy reserves dangerously low. He needed to get back home, to regroup and plan his next move.

But first, he needed to deal with Emma.

The walk back to his house was slow and painful. When Lucas arrived, he found Emma sitting on his porch, her arms wrapped tightly around herself. She looked up as he approached, her expression a mix of fear, confusion, and anger.

"Are you going to tell me what the hell just happened?" she demanded, standing as he climbed the steps.

Lucas sighed, his human form flickering back into place. His glowing eyes dulled, his elongated frame shrinking into something familiar. He looked at her, his face weary.

"You deserve the truth," he said finally. "But it's not going to be easy to hear."

Emma crossed her arms. "Try me."

Lucas hesitated, then nodded. "Let's go inside."

As they stepped into the dimly lit house, Lucas realized something had changed. For years, he had lived in the shadows, keeping his true nature hidden from everyone. But tonight, the shadows had been pulled back, and there was no going back.

For better or worse, his secret was out.

CHAPTER FIVE

The Truth Unveiled

The air inside Lucas's house was heavy with unspoken tension. Emma sat on the worn couch, her eyes scanning the room as though it might hold more secrets than the one standing in front of her. Lucas stood by the window, peering out into the quiet street. The battle in the forest might have ended, but the hunters' presence weighed on him. They would return—it was only a matter of time.

"You're going to have to start talking," Emma said, breaking the silence. Her voice was steady, but her grip on her flashlight betrayed the fear coursing through her.

Lucas sighed, pulling a chair from the dining table and sitting across from her. He rested his elbows on his knees, his hands clasped together. For a moment, he considered lying, spinning a story that might keep her at bay. But that wasn't an option anymore.

"I'm not from here," he began, his voice low.

Emma raised an eyebrow. "Not from Evergreen?"

Lucas shook his head. "Not from Earth."

The words hung in the air like a thunderclap. Emma stared at him, her expression shifting from disbelief to cautious curiosity. "You're serious," she said finally.

Lucas nodded. "My real name is Zarneth. I come from a planet called Vyrkos, light-years from here. I've been living on Earth for the past thirty years, hiding."

"Hiding from what?" Emma asked, leaning forward.

"From them," Lucas said, his gaze darkening. "The ones you saw in the forest. They're Vyrkani enforcers, hunters sent to track me down."

Emma took a deep breath, her mind racing. "Why? What did you do?"

Lucas hesitated. "I defied them. On Vyrkos, power and conquest are everything. My people dominate weaker planets, stripping them of resources and enslaving their inhabitants. I couldn't be part of it anymore, so I ran."

"And they've been chasing you ever since," Emma said, piecing it together.

Lucas nodded. "Earth was supposed to be safe. It's off their radar—insignificant, by their standards. But they've found me now, and they won't stop until I'm dead."

Emma sat back, processing everything. It was insane, impossible, yet she couldn't deny what she had seen in the forest. The glowing energy, the alien forms, the way Lucas had transformed—it was all too real.

"Why stay here?" she asked finally. "Why not keep moving?"

"I tried that at first," Lucas admitted. "But constantly running wears you down. I thought if I stayed long enough in one place, I could disappear, blend in. Evergreen felt... safe."

Emma shook her head, incredulous. "Safe? You've been hiding in plain sight, Lucas. And now those things are here, threatening this town."

"I know," Lucas said, his voice tinged with regret. "And I never wanted anyone else to be involved. That's why I've stayed distant, why I've kept to myself. But now..."

He trailed off, his thoughts heavy. Now, there was no more hiding.

Emma watched him, her reporter instincts warring with her sense of self-preservation. She had spent her career chasing stories, uncovering truths. But this—this was beyond anything she'd ever imagined. She should be terrified, running for the hills. Instead, she felt a strange pull, a determination to see this through.

"What happens next?" she asked, her voice quieter now.

Lucas met her gaze, his expression serious. "They'll come back. The enforcers won't stop until they've captured or killed me. And if the town gets in their way, they won't hesitate to destroy it."

Emma swallowed hard. "So, what do we do?"

"We?" Lucas asked, a hint of surprise in his voice.

Emma stood, crossing her arms. "You think I'm just going to walk away from this? Lucas, I'm already in it, whether I like it or not. You're not fighting this alone."

A flicker of something passed through Lucas's eyes—relief, perhaps, or gratitude. He gave a small nod. "We'll need to prepare. I have to figure out how to stop them before they call reinforcements."

Emma tilted her head. "Reinforcements?"

"The hunters are just the beginning," Lucas explained. "If they signal back to Vyrkos, they'll send more. An entire fleet, if necessary."

Emma's stomach turned. "So, we have to stop them from calling home."

"Exactly," Lucas said. "But that won't be easy. They're stronger, better equipped. And I can't fight them alone."

Emma bit her lip, thinking. "Then we don't fight them alone. There are people in this town who'd help, if they knew the truth."

"No." Lucas's response was immediate, his tone firm. "The more people who know, the greater the risk. The hunters will target anyone who gets in their way. I won't let that happen."

Emma hesitated, then nodded. "Okay. So, what do we do?"

Lucas stood, his determination hardening into resolve. "First, we track them. We need to find their base and disable their signal device before they can call for backup."

Emma frowned. "And how do we do that?"

Lucas tapped the small sphere he had used earlier, which now sat on the table. "This device can detect their energy fields. It'll lead us to them."

Emma looked at the sphere, then back at Lucas. "And then?"

Lucas's eyes glowed faintly, a reminder of the power he had been suppressing for so long. "Then we end this."

Outside, the forest was silent, the night air heavy with tension. Somewhere in the shadows, the hunters were regrouping, their mission far from over. But Lucas was done running. For the first time in decades, he was ready to fight back.

And this time, he wasn't alone.

CHAPTER SIX

Into the Shadows

The forest was a different world at night. The trees loomed tall and silent, their branches casting jagged shadows across the ground. The only sound was the faint crunch of leaves beneath Lucas's boots and the occasional rustle of wildlife moving unseen through the underbrush. He walked ahead of Emma, his every sense on high alert. The small spherical device in his hand pulsed with a faint blue glow, guiding them deeper into the woods.

"Are you sure this is a good idea?" Emma asked, her voice low but sharp. She struggled to keep pace with him, the flashlight in her hand barely cutting through the darkness.

"No," Lucas admitted. "But it's the only one we've got."

Emma huffed, not entirely reassured. She had seen enough to know Lucas wasn't like anyone else, but walking into the unknown with a glowing alien felt like tempting fate. Still, she followed. Something about him, about the way he carried himself, inspired a strange sort of trust—even when she didn't understand him.

"What exactly are we looking for?" she asked after a few minutes of silence.

"Their base," Lucas said without turning around. "They'll need somewhere to hide, to set up their equipment. Somewhere isolated."

Emma glanced around at the endless trees. "Well, they picked the right place."

Lucas didn't respond, his attention focused on the device in his hand. The pulses were growing stronger, more frequent. They were getting close.

After another mile, they reached a clearing. Lucas raised a hand, signaling Emma to stop. She froze, her flashlight trained on the ground as Lucas crouched low, scanning the area. The clearing was empty at first glance, but Lucas could feel the subtle hum of energy in the air. The hunters were here.

"What is it?" Emma whispered, crouching beside him.

Lucas pointed to the far side of the clearing. "There."

At first, Emma saw nothing. Then her eyes adjusted, and she caught a faint shimmer in the air, like heat rising off pavement. It was the same cloaking field she had seen before, but this one was larger, encompassing what looked like a series of metallic structures.

"What's inside?" she asked.

Lucas frowned. "Their equipment. Weapons. Maybe even their ship."

Emma swallowed hard. "And their signal device?"

"Most likely." Lucas stood, his gaze fixed on the shimmer. "If we can destroy it, they won't be able to call for reinforcements."

"And then?" Emma asked, her voice tinged with unease.

Lucas hesitated. "Then they'll have no choice but to leave—or face me."

Emma's stomach twisted. She didn't doubt Lucas's strength or his determination, but she had seen the hunters up close. They were efficient, lethal. Facing them seemed like a suicide mission.

"You have a plan for this, right?" she asked, forcing a shaky smile.

Lucas glanced at her, his expression serious. "I'm working on it."

As they crept closer to the clearing, Lucas studied the shimmering barrier, his mind racing. The hunters' cloaking field wasn't perfect—its edges flickered faintly, and the pulse of energy from the device in his hand confirmed that it was tied to a central power source. If he could locate and disable that source, the field would drop, exposing the base.

But doing so without being noticed was another matter entirely.

"Stay here," he said, handing Emma the device.

"What? No way," she protested, gripping the sphere tightly.

"Emma, if they see us both, we won't stand a chance," Lucas said, his tone firm. "I need you to stay out of sight. If anything goes wrong, get back to town and warn them."

Emma clenched her jaw, clearly torn. Finally, she nodded. "Fine. But if you get yourself killed, I'm not letting you off the hook."

Lucas gave her a faint smile. "Noted."

Lucas moved like a shadow, his movements fluid and silent. He slipped past the edge of the cloaking field, his heightened senses guiding him toward the source of the energy. The field crackled faintly as he passed through it, the metallic structures inside coming into view.

The base was small but efficient. A makeshift camp of sleek, black-metal equipment surrounded a central tower that pulsed with faint light. At the base of the tower, two hunters stood guard, their tall, angular forms silhouetted against the glow.

Lucas crouched behind a stack of crates, his mind racing. The tower was the key—it housed the signal device. If he could reach it without alerting the guards, he might be able to disable it before they realized what was happening.

But just as he began to move, a faint sound made him freeze.

Behind him, Emma crouched low, her flashlight off, her heart pounding. She had waited for all of five minutes before deciding she couldn't let Lucas face this alone. Watching him disappear into the shimmering field had sent a jolt of fear through her, and despite his orders, she had followed.

Now, she was regretting it.

She had barely stepped through the barrier when she heard the whir of machinery behind her. She turned slowly, her breath catching as one of the hunters emerged from the shadows, its glowing eyes locking onto her.

Emma swallowed hard. "Lucas?" she whispered, her voice barely audible.

The hunter raised its weapon.

Lucas felt it before he heard it—the ripple of energy as the hunter prepared to fire. He spun around, his eyes widening as he saw Emma standing frozen in the hunter's sights.

"Emma!" he shouted, breaking cover.

The hunter fired, and Lucas moved instinctively, a surge of energy propelling him forward. He reached Emma just in time, pulling her to the ground as the blast hit the crates behind them, sending shards of metal flying.

The guards by the tower turned at the commotion, their weapons raised.

"Run!" Lucas yelled, pushing Emma toward the edge of the field.

But Emma didn't move. She grabbed the device he had given her, thrusting it into his hands. "You said this would lead you to the signal. Use it!"

Lucas hesitated for a split second, then nodded. "Stay low."

He stood, his form shimmering as his human disguise melted away. His true self emerged, glowing and fierce, as he faced the hunters. Energy crackled around him as he raised a hand, sending a wave of force that knocked one of the guards off its feet.

The other hunter fired, its weapon's blast barely missing Lucas as he dodged. He sprinted toward the tower, the device in his hand pulsing wildly. The signal source was just ahead.

Emma watched in stunned silence as Lucas fought. He moved like a force of nature, his every movement precise and powerful. But the hunters were relentless, their weapons firing in rapid succession, each blast tearing through the clearing.

As Lucas reached the base of the tower, Emma saw one of the hunters breaking off, heading straight for him. Her heart pounded. She couldn't just sit there.

Grabbing a shard of metal from the wreckage, she ran after the hunter, shouting to draw its attention. It turned, momentarily distracted, and Emma swung with all her strength, the makeshift weapon striking its arm.

The hunter staggered, its weapon clattering to the ground. Emma didn't wait for it to recover. She ran toward Lucas, who was frantically dismantling the signal device at the base of the tower.

"Almost there!" he shouted, sparks flying as he worked.

The hunters regrouped, closing in. Lucas looked up, his glowing eyes meeting Emma's. "Get ready to run."

And then, with one final surge of energy, the tower exploded.

CHAPTER SEVEN

The Fallout

The explosion lit up the night, a searing flash that sent shockwaves rippling through the forest. Lucas and Emma were thrown to the ground, the force of the blast knocking the air from their lungs. For a brief moment, everything was silent, as though the world had paused to process what had just happened.

Lucas groaned, pushing himself up onto his elbows. His body ached, but he'd endured worse. The signal tower was gone, reduced to smoldering debris, and the shimmering cloaking field had collapsed. The hunters' base was fully exposed now, its metallic structures glowing faintly in the aftermath of the explosion.

"Emma?" Lucas called, his voice hoarse.

A few feet away, Emma stirred, coughing as she rolled onto her side. "Still here," she managed, her voice shaky. "That... was intense."

Lucas helped her to her feet, his glowing eyes scanning the clearing. The hunters were still alive. Two of them stood amidst the wreckage, their movements disoriented but quickly regaining composure. One had lost its weapon in the blast, while the other clutched a damaged device sparking at the seams.

"We have to go," Lucas said, gripping Emma's arm.

She nodded, her legs unsteady but moving. Together, they sprinted toward the tree line, the hunters' guttural shouts echoing behind them. Energy blasts seared the air around them, narrowly missing as they weaved through the forest.

They didn't stop running until the forest grew darker, quieter, and the sounds of pursuit faded into the distance. Lucas finally slowed, breathing heavily as he leaned against a tree. Emma collapsed onto the ground, her chest heaving.

"Are they... still coming?" she panted, looking back into the shadows.

"Not yet," Lucas replied, his voice tense. "The explosion disrupted their systems. They'll need time to regroup."

Emma wiped a hand across her forehead, smearing dirt and sweat. "Well, that was fun," she muttered. "Let's never do it again."

Lucas allowed himself a faint smile, despite the gravity of their situation. "You did good back there."

Emma glanced up at him, her expression a mixture of disbelief and sarcasm. "Yeah? Because I feel like I just nearly died a dozen times."

"You did," Lucas said, his tone serious. "But you also slowed them down. Without that, we wouldn't have made it out."

Emma stared at him for a moment, then sighed. "Great. Hero of the night. Now what?"

Lucas straightened, his mind already racing. The signal tower was destroyed, which meant the hunters couldn't call for reinforcements. But that didn't make them any less dangerous. They were still here, and they would stop at nothing to complete their mission.

"We need to regroup," Lucas said. "Rest, plan our next move."

Emma raised an eyebrow. "Rest? You? I thought you were some invincible alien warrior."

Lucas shook his head, a wry smile tugging at his lips. "Far from it. Using my abilities drains me, just like anything else. If I push too hard, I could burn out completely."

Emma frowned, a hint of concern crossing her face. "Well, that's... reassuring."

Lucas crouched beside her, his glowing eyes dimming slightly as his energy settled. "Emma, I need you to understand something. The hunters aren't going to stop. We've bought some time, but they'll come after us—and the town—again. We have to be ready."

Emma nodded slowly, her resolve hardening. "Okay. So what do we do?"

Lucas hesitated. The next step wasn't just about survival—it was about making sure the hunters couldn't hurt anyone else. "We find their ship," he said finally. "Destroy it. Without it, they'll be stranded here."

Emma's eyes widened. "Stranded? Like you?"

Lucas nodded. "They'll have no way back to Vyrkos. No way to report. It's the only way to end this."

Emma sat back, her expression thoughtful. "And what happens to them after that?"

"They'll have no choice but to assimilate," Lucas said. "Blend in, like I have. They won't be able to use their abilities without drawing attention."

Emma tilted her head. "That's a big gamble, isn't it? What if they decide to start taking over anyway?"

Lucas's jaw tightened. "Then I'll stop them."

The determination in his voice sent a shiver down Emma's spine. She realized just how much weight Lucas carried, how much he had sacrificed to protect a world that wasn't even his own. And now, he was willing to risk everything to keep it safe.

"All right," she said, standing. "Let's find that ship."

The journey back to town was slow and cautious. Lucas kept his senses sharp, scanning for any sign of pursuit. The hunters were still out there, but for now, the forest remained quiet. By the time they reached the edge of Evergreen, dawn was breaking, painting the sky in soft hues of pink and orange.

They slipped into Lucas's house, closing the door quietly behind them. Emma sank onto the couch, exhausted, while Lucas moved to the window, peering out at the empty street.

"You should get some rest," he said without turning around.

Emma snorted. "Right. Because sleep is totally happening after all that."

Lucas glanced back at her, his expression softening. "You'll need your strength for what's coming."

She sighed, rubbing her temples. "I can't believe this is my life now. A week ago, I was chasing rumors about power outages. Now I'm... what? Fighting aliens?"

Lucas smiled faintly. "Welcome to my world."

Emma met his gaze, and for a moment, the weight of the situation lifted. They had survived the night, and for now, that was enough.

But deep in the forest, the hunters were already regrouping. The loss of the signal tower had slowed them, but it hadn't stopped them. Their leader, taller and more imposing than the others, surveyed the wreckage with cold, glowing eyes.

"This changes nothing," it growled in its native tongue. "Zarneth will not escape."

The others nodded, their movements sharp and precise. The leader turned its gaze toward the horizon, where the faint lights of Evergreen glimmered in the distance.

"Prepare the ship," it ordered. "We end this soon."

CHAPTER EIGHT

The Ship

The forest grew darker as Lucas and Emma approached the edge of the ravine. The air was heavy, charged with an almost electric hum that set Emma's teeth on edge. Ahead, the alien ship loomed, a sleek, obsidian monolith crouching like a predator in the shadows. Its surface shimmered faintly, reflecting the sparse moonlight, and a thin mist seemed to rise around it, unnatural and unnerving.

Emma stopped, her breath hitching. "That's it, isn't it?"

Lucas didn't answer immediately. He was staring at the ship, his glowing eyes narrowing as he scanned its contours. The ship wasn't just advanced—it was alive in its own way, pulsing faintly with energy that resonated with his own. He could feel it in his bones, the deep thrum of its power core calling to him like a heartbeat.

"It's not just a ship," he said finally. "It's their anchor. Their strength."

Emma shivered. "How do we even get near that thing?"

Lucas knelt, pulling out the spherical tracking device. Its blue glow intensified, casting long shadows across the ground. "The ship's energy field is strongest at the center. If we can reach the core, we can overload it."

Emma stared at him. "And by 'overload,' you mean blow it to pieces?"

"Exactly," Lucas said, tucking the device back into his pocket. "But we'll have to be careful. They'll have defenses, and if they catch us—"

"They won't," Emma interrupted, surprising herself with her conviction. "We've come this far. We're not stopping now."

Lucas glanced at her, a flicker of admiration crossing his face. "Stay close," he said. "And stay quiet."

They descended into the ravine, the rocky terrain shifting under their feet. Emma struggled to keep her footing, but Lucas moved with inhuman grace, his senses attuned to every sound and movement. As they neared the ship, Emma realized just how massive it was. What she had seen from above was only a fragment; the rest of the vessel extended deep into the earth, its metallic hull covered in intricate patterns that seemed to pulse with their own light.

"It's beautiful," she murmured, then immediately regretted it.

"Beautiful and deadly," Lucas replied. "Don't let it distract you."

Emma swallowed hard. As they crept closer, the hum of the ship grew louder, vibrating through the ground and up her legs. The air felt thicker here, harder to breathe. She glanced at Lucas, who seemed unaffected, his glowing form casting faint halos of light onto the surrounding rock.

He held up a hand, stopping her. "Guards."

Emma followed his gaze. Two hunters stood at the base of the ship, their elongated forms shrouded in shadow. They were motionless, their glowing eyes fixed on the surrounding area, scanning for threats.

"What now?" Emma whispered, gripping the flashlight in her pocket.

Lucas tilted his head, calculating. "I'll take them out. Wait here."

"Wait—" Emma started, but Lucas was already moving.

Lucas moved like a shadow, his form rippling as he shed the last traces of his human disguise. His glowing skin blended with the faint light of the ship, making him almost invisible as he closed the distance. Emma watched, her heart pounding, as he approached the first hunter. There was no sound, no warning—just a flash of movement as Lucas struck, his energy crackling as it connected.

The hunter crumpled silently. The second turned, raising its weapon, but Lucas was faster. He ducked under the blast, the energy searing the air where he had stood, and countered with a precise strike to the hunter's chest. The creature staggered, its armor sparking, before collapsing in a heap.

Lucas stood over them for a moment, his glowing eyes scanning for any signs of life. Satisfied, he motioned for Emma to join him.

"Show-off," she muttered as she approached, but there was no malice in her tone.

"Let's move," Lucas said, already turning toward the ship.

The entry hatch hissed open as they approached, its edges glowing faintly. Inside, the ship was eerily quiet. The walls pulsed with faint light, casting shifting patterns across the floor. Emma hesitated at the threshold, her instincts screaming at her to turn back.

"It's... alive," she said, her voice barely above a whisper.

"Not alive," Lucas corrected. "Responsive. It's tuned to their energy, their biology. We're intruders here."

"Great," Emma muttered, stepping inside. "Love being an intruder."

The interior of the ship was unlike anything Emma had ever seen. The corridors were sleek and seamless, as though the entire structure had been carved from a single piece of metal. Strange symbols glowed faintly on the walls, shifting and changing as they moved. Emma reached out to touch one, but Lucas grabbed her wrist.

"Don't," he said sharply. "The ship reacts to touch. It could alert them."

Emma nodded, pulling her hand back. "Got it. No touching the glowing alien symbols."

Lucas smirked faintly. "Good rule."

As they moved deeper into the ship, the hum of the power core grew louder, the air vibrating with its intensity. Lucas stopped at a junction, his glowing eyes narrowing.

"It's close," he said, gesturing down one of the corridors. "The core will be heavily guarded. Stay behind me."

Emma nodded, clutching the flashlight in her pocket. Her heart was pounding, but she forced herself to stay calm. They had made it this far. There was no turning back.

The core chamber was massive, a cathedral of light and energy. At its center was a sphere of pulsing, brilliant light, suspended in midair by streams of crackling energy. The conduits feeding into it glowed with shifting colors, their patterns hypnotic.

But what caught Emma's attention was the figure standing in front of the core. Taller than the other hunters, its form was sleeker, its armor darker. Its eyes glowed brighter, and it radiated an aura of authority.

"The leader," Lucas said under his breath.

The leader turned as they entered, its glowing eyes narrowing. "Zarneth," it said, its voice deep and guttural. "You've come far, only to fail."

Lucas stepped forward, his glowing form pulsing with energy. "You don't belong here. Leave, or face the consequences."

The leader laughed, a sound like grinding metal. "You are outnumbered and outmatched. This world will fall, just as so many others have."

Lucas didn't respond. He raised his hands, and the air between them crackled with energy. The leader mirrored the motion, its own energy surging as it prepared to strike.

"Lucas—" Emma started, but the battle had already begun.

The chamber erupted into chaos. Lucas and the leader clashed, their energy blasts colliding in brilliant explosions that shook the walls. The conduits feeding the core sparked wildly, the power levels rising as the fight raged on.

Emma ducked behind a console, her eyes darting between the battle and the core. The sphere was glowing brighter, its cracks spreading as the energy surged. She realized what was happening: the fight was destabilizing the core.

"Lucas!" she shouted. "The core—"

"I know!" he called back, dodging a blast from the leader. "Get out of here!"

Emma ignored him. Instead, she looked at the console in front of her, its symbols glowing faintly. She didn't understand them, but she didn't need to. If the core was already destabilizing, she could push it over the edge.

"Emma, no!" Lucas shouted, but it was too late.

Emma slammed her hand onto the console. The symbols flared, and the core let out a deafening roar. The energy surged, the sphere fracturing as light poured from its cracks.

The leader turned, its glowing eyes widening. "No!"

Lucas sprinted toward Emma, grabbing her just as the core exploded.

The shockwave threw them both from the ship, the force of the blast flattening the trees around the ravine. Lucas shielded Emma with his body, absorbing the brunt of the energy as they tumbled to the ground.

When the dust settled, Emma opened her eyes to find Lucas lying beside her, his glowing form flickering.

"You okay?" he asked, his voice weak.

Emma coughed, her head spinning. "Yeah. You?"

Lucas managed a faint smile. "I've been worse."

The ship was gone, reduced to a smoldering crater. The hunters had no way off the planet now, no way to call for reinforcements. For the first time in decades, Lucas felt a glimmer of hope.

"We did it," Emma said, her voice soft.

Lucas nodded, his gaze fixed on the rising sun. "For now."

CHAPTER NINE

The Price of Survival

The smoldering crater where the ship had been was still releasing faint wisps of smoke as Lucas and Emma lay in the wreckage of the ravine. The morning sunlight pierced through the trees, highlighting the ash-streaked faces of the unlikely pair. The silence was deafening, the hum of alien energy finally extinguished.

Lucas sat up slowly, his glowing form flickering like a candle on its last wick. The fight had taken everything out of him, and he felt as though he'd aged a century in the last hour. Emma groaned beside him, holding her ribs as she tried to push herself upright.

"You're insane," she muttered, coughing through the words. "And I think I'm officially insane for following you."

Lucas allowed himself a faint smile. "You volunteered."

"Yeah, remind me to stop doing that," Emma said, wincing as she shifted. Her eyes darted to the crater, now blackened and lifeless. "So... it's over?"

"For now," Lucas said, his tone cautious. "The ship is destroyed, and the core explosion would've wiped out most of their equipment. But the hunters are still alive."

Emma stiffened. "How do you know?"

"They're Vyrkani," Lucas explained. "They wouldn't go down that easily. They'll regroup, but without their ship, their options are limited. They'll either assimilate... or retaliate."

Emma glanced at him sharply. "Retaliate? Against the town?"

"It's possible," Lucas admitted, his gaze distant. "But we've crippled their mission. They have no reinforcements, no way off the planet. Their survival depends on staying hidden."

Emma's stomach twisted. "So we're back to square one. Only now, they're desperate."

Lucas didn't respond. He stood slowly, his glowing eyes scanning the forest for signs of movement. The morning light made him look almost human again, but Emma couldn't shake the image of him in the ship, his alien form blazing with power. He was otherworldly, yes, but he had risked everything for her—and for this town.

The walk back to Evergreen was slow and tense. Every rustle of leaves, every snap of a branch made them stop and listen, their nerves frayed from the night's events. Lucas led the way, his senses sharp, but the hunters had gone silent.

When they finally reached the edge of town, Emma collapsed onto a park bench, her legs giving out beneath her. "We made it," she breathed, wiping sweat from her brow.

Lucas remained standing, his gaze fixed on the distant tree line. "For now."

Emma looked up at him, her brow furrowing. "You keep saying that. For now, for now. When does this end, Lucas? When can we stop looking over our shoulders?"

Lucas hesitated. "When they're gone. Or when I am."

Emma's heart sank. "Don't say that."

"It's the truth," Lucas said quietly. "I'm the reason they're here. If I disappear, the town might be safe."

Emma stood abruptly, anger flaring in her chest. "You think sacrificing yourself is the answer? That's not happening, Lucas. Not after everything we've been through."

Lucas met her gaze, his glowing eyes softening. "Emma—"

"No," she interrupted, stepping closer. "We fight them together. We've made it this far. You don't get to throw yourself on the sword now.”

Lucas studied her for a long moment, then nodded. “All right. Together.”

As the sun climbed higher, the town began to wake. Families opened their curtains, kids rode their bikes in the streets, and Evergreen returned to its quiet normalcy. But for Lucas and Emma, normal was no longer an option.

Back at Lucas's house, the weight of the night's events settled over them like a storm cloud. Scout greeted them at the door, her tail wagging weakly as she sniffed at Lucas's soot-covered pants. He knelt to pet her, his touch gentle despite his exhaustion.

Emma sank into the couch, her head in her hands. "What now?" she asked after a long silence.

"We prepare," Lucas said, sitting across from her. "The hunters won't stay quiet for long. They'll need resources, a new base. We have to find them before they recover."

Emma groaned. "Can we at least get a few hours of sleep first?"

Lucas allowed himself a faint smile. "You've earned it."

But sleep didn't come easily. While Emma dozed fitfully on the couch, Lucas sat by the window, his glowing eyes scanning the street. The hunters were wounded, scattered, but they were still dangerous. He had no doubt they would strike again—whether out of desperation or revenge, he couldn't say.

He thought of Emma, her stubborn determination and quick wit. She had risked her life for him, for a cause she barely understood. She didn't owe him anything, yet she had stayed. And now, she was a target because of him.

Lucas clenched his fists. He wouldn't let the hunters take this town. Not Emma. Not anyone.

Deep in the forest, the hunters regrouped. The leader stood at the edge of the crater, its glowing eyes narrowing as it surveyed the wreckage. The ship was gone, their mission compromised, but its resolve remained unshaken.

"This isn't over," it growled, its voice echoing through the trees.

The others nodded silently, their angular forms casting long shadows in the dim light. They had lost their ship, their signal device, but they still had their weapons. And they still had their target.

"Zarneth will pay," the leader said, its tone cold and final. "And the humans will suffer for their defiance."

The hunters dispersed, their movements swift and silent. The hunt was far from over.

CHAPTER TEN

Shadows in the Town

Lucas hadn't slept in two days. The hunters were regrouping; he could feel it, like an electric pulse running through the air. Each passing hour brought a sharper edge to his instincts, urging him to act before they did. But where? How? The hunters were masters of stealth, and Evergreen was a sprawling maze of streets, forests, and secluded spaces where they could hide.

Emma stirred on the couch, her movements slow and deliberate as she sat up. "Still brooding by the window?" she asked, her voice thick with exhaustion.

Lucas turned to her, his glowing eyes dim in the soft morning light. "I can't afford to stop."

Emma stretched, wincing as her ribs protested. "You know, humans have this thing called 'rest.' You should try it."

Lucas gave her a faint smile but didn't reply. He looked back out the window. The world outside appeared normal—kids riding bikes, a dog barking in the distance, someone mowing their lawn. But beneath the surface, something was brewing. The hunters weren't just hiding. They were watching.

"We can't wait for them to make the first move," Lucas said finally. "We have to find them."

Emma rubbed her temples, her frustration evident. "How? We destroyed their ship, their signal. They're probably just licking their wounds in some cave."

"No," Lucas said, his tone sharp. "They're planning something. And we're running out of time."

The Tracker Returns

Lucas placed the small spherical device on the table. It had been instrumental in finding the ship, but its energy signature had weakened significantly after the explosion. He turned it over in his hands, his fingers brushing against the smooth surface as he searched for a way to reactivate it.

"Is that thing still working?" Emma asked, leaning closer.

"Barely," Lucas admitted. "The core explosion disrupted its calibration, but it should still pick up residual energy if we're close enough."

Emma watched him work, her brows furrowed. "Close enough to what? What are we even looking for?"

"The hunters are scattered, but they'll need a central location to regroup," Lucas said. "They'll want to reestablish some kind of power base."

Emma's stomach sank. "And you think they're doing that... here? In Evergreen?"

Lucas nodded. "They have no other choice. They need resources—electricity, materials, food. They'll blend in, just like I did."

The thought sent a chill down Emma's spine. The hunters, hiding among the townspeople, invisible and dangerous. "How will we know who they are?"

Lucas glanced at her, his expression grim. "We'll know."

The Town Meeting

Later that day, Lucas and Emma walked into town, the tension between them palpable. Lucas had suggested they observe the townspeople, searching for any unusual behavior that might indicate the hunters' presence. Emma had reluctantly agreed, though she couldn't shake the feeling that they were grasping at straws.

Evergreen's town square was bustling with activity. A small farmers' market had sprung up, and families strolled between stalls, chatting and laughing. To anyone else, it was a picture-perfect day. But Lucas's sharp eyes scanned the crowd, his senses tuned to the slightest anomaly.

"See anything?" Emma asked, her voice low.

"Not yet," Lucas replied, his gaze darting from face to face. Most of the people moved naturally, their body language easy and relaxed. But as his eyes swept over the far side of the square, he froze.

A man stood by a stall, his movements stiff and deliberate. He didn't engage with the vendor or the other customers. Instead, he seemed to be scanning the crowd, his head moving in sharp, precise motions.

"Over there," Lucas said, nodding toward the man.

Emma followed his gaze, her heart skipping a beat. "You think...?"

Lucas's jaw tightened. "I'm sure of it."

A Confrontation

Lucas and Emma trailed the man as he left the market, their movements careful and deliberate. He walked with a purpose, his path taking him toward the outskirts of town. Lucas kept a safe distance, his senses on high alert.

The man turned down a narrow alley, and Lucas quickened his pace. "Stay back," he whispered to Emma.

"Not a chance," she hissed, following him anyway.

As they rounded the corner, the man stopped abruptly, his back to them. The air seemed to grow heavier, charged with an unseen energy. Slowly, the man turned, his glowing eyes locking onto Lucas.

"Zarneth," the hunter growled, its human disguise rippling as it shed its form. The creature that emerged was tall and angular, its dark armor gleaming faintly in the dim light.

Lucas stepped forward, his own form shifting as his glowing skin illuminated the narrow alley. "It's over," he said, his voice steady. "Your mission is done."

The hunter laughed, a cold, metallic sound. "You destroyed the ship, but we are not defeated. This world will fall, and you with it."

Before Lucas could respond, the hunter lunged, its movements a blur. Lucas met the attack head-on, their clash sending shockwaves through the alley. Emma pressed herself against the wall, her heart racing as the two beings fought.

Lucas moved with precision, his energy crackling as he deflected the hunter's strikes. But the creature was relentless, its attacks fueled by rage and desperation. It struck Lucas with a powerful blow, sending him crashing into the wall.

"Lucas!" Emma shouted, her voice breaking.

The hunter turned toward her, its glowing eyes narrowing. "The human," it sneered. "Your weakness."

Emma's breath caught in her throat as the creature advanced. But before it could reach her, Lucas surged forward, his energy blazing as he tackled the hunter to the ground.

"Run!" Lucas shouted, his voice echoing through the alley.

Emma hesitated for only a second before sprinting toward the square, her heart pounding. Behind her, the sounds of the battle grew fainter, replaced by the distant hum of the town.

A Glimpse of Hope

When Emma reached the safety of the square, she stopped, gasping for breath. She turned back toward the alley, her mind racing. Lucas had told her to run, but she couldn't leave him. Not like this.

Just as she was about to return, Lucas emerged, his form flickering as he stumbled into the light. His face was bruised, and his movements were unsteady, but he was alive.

"You okay?" Emma asked, rushing to his side.

Lucas nodded, though his expression was grim. "The hunter is gone—for now. But this isn't over."

Emma swallowed hard. "What do we do?"

Lucas looked at her, his glowing eyes filled with resolve. "We find the others. We finish this."

CHAPTER ELEVEN

Hiding in Plain Sight

Evergreen felt different now, even in the golden light of morning. For Emma, the quiet streets and friendly faces of her neighbors seemed shrouded in suspicion. Every passerby could be hiding something, every friendly smile a mask. The hunters were somewhere out there, blending in, and the weight of that knowledge pressed heavily on her.

Lucas walked beside her, his movements purposeful yet subdued. His human form, with those piercing blue eyes flecked with gold, was back in place, but Emma had seen beyond the mask. She now understood the strength and fragility he balanced every day. The task ahead of them—rooting out the hunters before they could retaliate—seemed impossibly daunting.

"Where do we start?" Emma asked as they turned down Main Street. The town square buzzed with life: vendors selling produce, children laughing, the hum of distant lawnmowers. It was hard to imagine such a serene setting hiding an alien threat.

Lucas scanned the area, his eyes sharp. "We watch. They'll need resources, and they'll leave traces if they're desperate enough. The hunters can't hide their nature forever."

Emma frowned, her gaze sweeping the crowd. "You're telling me to just... spot the alien in a crowd? Isn't that, you know, kind of impossible?"

Lucas gave her a sidelong glance. "It's not as hard as you think. Their movements—too precise. Their emotions—detached. They observe, but they don't connect."

Emma folded her arms, skeptical. "Great. So we're looking for the most socially awkward people in town?"

Lucas didn't respond, his attention drawn to a group of people gathered near a coffee stand. One man stood apart, his posture rigid, his expression blank as he watched the interactions around him. His movements were slow, deliberate, as if he were analyzing every detail.

"There," Lucas said, nodding toward the man. "Do you see it?"

Emma squinted, studying the man. At first glance, he seemed normal—tall, slightly pale, with nondescript clothing. But the longer she watched, the more unsettling he seemed. He never spoke, never moved closer to the group. His eyes were fixed on the people in front of him, unblinking.

"He's just... standing there," Emma said. "Like he doesn't know how to be part of the crowd."

Lucas nodded. "Exactly."

A Dangerous Approach

Lucas moved toward the man, his steps measured, his expression calm. Emma followed reluctantly, her heart pounding. She wasn't sure what Lucas planned to do, but the tension in his movements suggested this wasn't just observation anymore.

The man noticed them as they approached, his eyes flicking to Lucas. Something shifted in his posture—a subtle tensing, like a predator preparing to strike. Lucas stopped a few feet away, his voice low and even.

"Nice day," he said.

The man tilted his head, his eyes narrowing slightly. "Yes. It is."

The words were flat, mechanical, devoid of the warmth or rhythm of human speech. Emma's breath caught. There was no mistaking it now—this wasn't just an odd stranger. This was one of them.

Lucas kept his voice calm. "I don't think we've met. I'm Lucas."

The man's gaze lingered on Lucas for a moment too long. "David," he said finally, the name sounding foreign in his mouth.

Emma stepped forward, forcing a smile. "David? I think I've seen you around. Are you new in town?"

David's gaze shifted to her, his expression unreadable. "I've been here. Watching."

Emma suppressed a shiver, her heart racing. "Well, if you need anything, let us know. Everyone here is pretty friendly."

David's lips curved into what might have been an attempt at a smile, but it was unsettling, his teeth too perfectly aligned, his expression too calculated. "Thank you."

Lucas stepped closer, his tone low and firm. "We'll be seeing you, David."

David's eyes flicked back to Lucas, narrowing slightly. For a brief moment, the air between them seemed to hum with tension, an unspoken challenge passing between the two. Then David turned and walked away, his movements precise and unhurried.

A Fractured Peace

Emma waited until David was out of sight before turning to Lucas. "That was him, wasn't it?"

Lucas nodded, his expression grim. "One of them."

"What do we do?" Emma asked, her voice tight. "Do we follow him? Confront him?"

"Not yet," Lucas said. "He knows we've noticed him. That will make him cautious. He might lead us to the others."

Emma hesitated, her frustration bubbling over. "We can't just let him walk away, Lucas. He's dangerous."

"I know," Lucas said, his tone steady. "But rushing in without a plan will get us killed—and it'll put everyone else in danger. We have to be patient."

Emma clenched her fists, hating how much sense he made. "Fine. But the next time we see him, I'm not letting him out of my sight."

Lucas gave her a faint smile. "I wouldn't expect anything less."

Shadows Gather

That night, as the town settled into its usual quiet rhythm, Lucas and Emma sat in his living room, poring over a map of Evergreen. Lucas had marked areas where the hunters might be hiding—abandoned buildings, secluded lots, dense patches of forest. It was a long list, and each location felt like a potential trap.

"They're regrouping," Lucas said, tracing a finger along one of the forested areas near the edge of town. "They'll need to consolidate their resources before they strike again."

Emma leaned back, her arms crossed. "So we're just supposed to wait until they make their move?"

"Not wait," Lucas said. "Prepare."

Emma sighed, rubbing her temples. "This is so far out of my league, Lucas. I'm just a reporter. I don't know how to fight aliens."

"You're doing better than most would," Lucas said, his voice soft. "And you're not alone."

Emma glanced at him, surprised by the warmth in his tone. She didn't know what to say, so she simply nodded. For all her fear and doubt, she knew one thing: she couldn't walk away from this. Not now.

The Hunters' Plan

Deep in the forest, David returned to a hidden clearing where the remaining hunters were gathered. Their forms flickered faintly, their disguises unstable in the dim light. The leader stood at the center, its glowing eyes fixed on David as he approached.

"Report," the leader growled.

David inclined his head. "Zarneth is watching. He and the human know we are here."

The leader's gaze darkened. "Good. Let them watch. Let them think they have the upper hand."

The other hunters shifted, their movements restless. One stepped forward, its voice cold. "The ship is gone. Our resources are depleted. How do we strike?"

The leader's lips curled into a sinister smile. "We don't strike yet. We let them come to us. And when they do, we'll finish what we started."

The clearing fell silent, the hunters' glowing eyes gleaming in the darkness. The hunt was far from over.

CHAPTER TWELVE

The Silent Chase

Lucas spent the next morning tracking "David," following the faint trail of alien energy he left behind. The hunters couldn't fully suppress their presence; their advanced biology radiated subtle electromagnetic waves that Lucas could sense like ripples in a still pond. Emma walked a step behind, clutching a notepad in one hand and a flashlight in the other, despite the bright daylight.

"Do you really think he'll lead us to the others?" Emma asked, glancing nervously around the wooded path they were following.

"He has no choice," Lucas replied, his voice low. "Hunters aren't solitary. They'll regroup to consolidate resources, coordinate their next move. If we're lucky, he'll take us straight to their base."

Emma frowned, her steps faltering. "And if we're not lucky?"

Lucas didn't answer, his eyes fixed on the faint tracks in the dirt—a trail too clean, too perfect, as though someone had deliberately placed each step. It was a classic hunter tactic: lead the prey into a false sense of security before turning the tables. He stopped abruptly, holding up a hand to signal Emma to stay still.

"What?" she whispered, barely moving.

Lucas tilted his head, listening. The forest was unnaturally quiet. No birds, no rustling leaves—only the faint hum of something metallic. His glowing eyes narrowed as he scanned the area.

"They know we're following," he said softly. "They're setting a trap."

Emma's heart skipped a beat. "What do we do?"

Lucas straightened, his jaw tightening. "We spring it."

The Clearing

The trail led them to a small clearing surrounded by tall, gnarled trees. At the center stood David, his back to them. He was perfectly still, his rigid posture eerily unnatural. A faint mist clung to the ground, swirling around his feet like tendrils.

Lucas stepped into the clearing, his form shifting subtly as his alien instincts prepared for a fight. "David," he called, his voice calm but commanding.

David turned slowly, his glowing eyes meeting Lucas's. The human disguise rippled and faded, revealing the angular, armored form of the hunter beneath. He stood tall and imposing, his features sharp and mechanical, his gaze filled with cold calculation.

"Zarneth," David said, his voice guttural and echoing. "You've been busy."

Lucas didn't respond. He stepped forward, placing himself between David and Emma, who lingered at the edge of the clearing, her hand gripping the flashlight tightly.

David tilted his head, his expression unreadable. "You can't win, Zarneth. You're one. We are many."

Lucas's eyes narrowed. "You're stranded. You have no reinforcements, no resources. You can't hide forever."

David's lips curled into a sinister smile. "We don't need to hide. This world will be ours, one way or another."

Before Lucas could respond, the ground beneath him shook violently. The air filled with a deafening hum as two more hunters stepped into the clearing, their forms flickering as they shed their disguises. They moved with inhuman precision, their glowing eyes fixed on Lucas.

Emma's breath caught. "Lucas—"

"Stay back!" Lucas barked, his voice sharp.

The hunters advanced, their movements coordinated and deliberate. Lucas shifted fully into his alien form, his glowing body radiating energy as he prepared to fight. The tension in the clearing was palpable, the air thick with the promise of violence.

The Fight

The first hunter lunged, its angular limbs slicing through the air. Lucas dodged, his movements fluid and precise, and countered with a blast of energy that sent the creature staggering back. The second hunter struck from the side, its clawed hand aiming for Lucas's throat. He caught the blow, his strength barely holding it at bay as the creature snarled.

David hung back, observing the fight with a calm, calculating demeanor. "You've grown weak, Zarneth," he said, his tone mocking. "Years of pretending to be human have dulled your edge."

Lucas didn't respond. He spun, throwing the second hunter into the first with a surge of force that sent both crashing into the trees. The impact shook the ground, but the hunters were relentless, rising immediately to continue their attack.

Emma stood frozen at the edge of the clearing, her heart pounding. She wanted to help, to do something, but what could she do against creatures like this? She gripped her flashlight tighter, her mind racing.

Suddenly, David turned his gaze toward her. "The human," he said, his voice dripping with disdain. "Your weakness."

Emma's stomach twisted as David began to advance. "Stay away from her!" Lucas shouted, breaking away from the other hunters.

But David was faster. He closed the distance between them in an instant, his glowing eyes locking onto Emma. She raised the flashlight instinctively, holding it like a weapon, even though she knew it would be useless.

"You don't belong in this fight," David said, his voice cold.

Emma's hand trembled, but she didn't back down. "Maybe not," she said, her voice trembling. "But I'm here anyway."

David raised his hand, a blade-like appendage emerging from his armor. Emma's breath caught, but before he could strike, Lucas slammed into him from the side, sending them both tumbling to the ground.

A Desperate Plan

The fight raged on, the clearing lit by flashes of energy as Lucas battled the hunters. Emma could only watch, her heart in her throat, as he fought with everything he had. But it was clear he was outnumbered, his movements slowing as exhaustion set in.

"We can't win this," Lucas said through gritted teeth, dodging another strikc. "We have to retreat."

Emma's mind raced. "How? They'll just follow us!"

Lucas's glowing eyes met hers, a flicker of desperation in their depths. "There's a cave system nearby. If we can collapse the entrance, it'll buy us time."

Emma hesitated, the weight of the plan sinking in. "And you think we can make it there?"

"We have to try," Lucas said, deflecting another blow.

Emma nodded, her fear replaced by a grim determination. "Lead the way."

The Escape

Lucas fought his way to Emma's side, his energy flaring as he forced the hunters back. "Run!" he shouted, grabbing her arm and pulling her toward the edge of the clearing.

They sprinted through the forest, the hunters close behind. The air was filled with the sound of breaking branches and snarls as their pursuers closed the gap. Emma's lungs burned, her legs screaming for relief, but she didn't stop. She couldn't.

The cave loomed ahead, its dark entrance a gaping maw in the hillside. Lucas shoved Emma inside, turning to face the hunters as they closed in.

"Start collapsing the entrance!" he shouted.

Emma grabbed a large rock, using all her strength to dislodge smaller stones and debris from the cave walls. The ground trembled as the hunters charged, their glowing eyes blazing with fury.

Lucas stood his ground, his energy crackling as he unleashed a powerful blast. The impact shook the cave, sending rocks tumbling from the ceiling. The hunters hesitated, their movements uncertain as the entrance began to cave in.

"Now!" Lucas shouted, his voice echoing.

Emma gave one final push, and the entrance collapsed in a thunderous roar, sealing them inside.

CHAPTER THIRTEEN

Trapped

The cave fell silent after the last rock settled into place. Dust hung heavy in the air, swirling in the faint beams of light that managed to seep through small cracks in the debris. Emma coughed, her voice muffled as she brushed dirt from her face. Her hands trembled, raw from the frantic effort to collapse the entrance.

"Lucas?" she called, her voice shaky but urgent.

"I'm here," Lucas replied, his glowing eyes cutting through the darkness as he moved toward her. He was battered and bruised, his form flickering faintly with the effort of maintaining his energy. "Are you hurt?"

Emma shook her head, though her body ached all over. "Just shaken. You?"

"I'll recover," Lucas said, though the strain in his voice betrayed him. "We bought ourselves some time, but not much."

Emma leaned against the cave wall, her breathing uneven. "They'll dig through eventually, won't they?"

Lucas nodded. "They will. But for now, we're safe."

"Safe?" Emma snapped, her voice rising. "We're trapped in a cave with no way out, and they're waiting for us on the other side! How is that safe?"

Lucas's gaze softened. "We're alive. That's enough for now."

Assessing the Situation

The cave stretched deeper into the hillside, its walls jagged and damp. Lucas led Emma farther inside, his glowing eyes casting a faint light as he scanned their surroundings. The air was cool, heavy with the scent of earth and moss.

"We need to keep moving," Lucas said, his tone firm. "If there's another exit, we have to find it before they do."

Emma followed reluctantly, her steps unsteady. "And if there isn't?"

"Then we make one," Lucas replied, though even he didn't sound convinced.

The cave narrowed as they walked, forcing them to move single file. Emma shivered as droplets of water dripped from the ceiling, the sound echoing in the otherwise silent passage. She tried to focus on putting one foot in front of the other, but her mind kept drifting to the hunters outside. They were relentless, and she couldn't shake the feeling that they were running out of options.

A Hidden Danger

As they ventured deeper, the cave began to widen again, opening into a larger chamber. Lucas stopped abruptly, his glowing eyes narrowing. Emma nearly ran into him.

"What is it?" she asked, her voice hushed.

Lucas raised a hand, motioning for her to stay quiet. The air in the chamber felt different—charged, almost alive. He stepped forward cautiously, his senses on high alert.

That's when he saw it.

In the center of the chamber stood a strange, pulsating structure. It was unlike anything Emma had ever seen, a mass of glowing tendrils and jagged metal fused into the rock. It emitted a faint hum, the sound resonating deep in her chest.

"What the hell is that?" Emma whispered, her voice trembling.

Lucas's expression darkened. "A relay."

Emma frowned. "A what?"

"It's how they've been coordinating," Lucas explained, stepping closer to the structure. "This isn't just a hiding spot—it's a base. They've embedded their technology into the cave."

Emma's stomach dropped. "So they've been here all along? Watching the town?"

Lucas nodded grimly. "And planning their next move."

The Relay's Purpose

Lucas examined the relay, his fingers brushing against the glowing tendrils. The structure pulsed faintly at his touch, almost as if it were alive. His expression grew more serious with each passing second.

"They're using this to communicate," he said finally. "Not with their homeworld—that signal was lost when we destroyed the ship. But with each other."

Emma's eyes widened. "You mean... there could be more of them?"

Lucas turned to her, his gaze heavy. "It's possible. This relay is meant to coordinate. It's designed to control, to issue commands. If we don't destroy it, they'll regroup and strike harder."

Emma stared at the relay, her heart pounding. "And how exactly do we destroy it?"

Lucas hesitated, his glowing eyes scanning the structure. "It's connected to the cave. If I can overload it, it'll collapse this entire section."

Emma stiffened. "The whole section? Including us?"

"I'll buy you time to get out," Lucas said, his voice calm but resolute.

Emma grabbed his arm, her grip firm. "No. We're not doing this 'heroic sacrifice' thing again, Lucas. There has to be another way."

Lucas met her gaze, his expression conflicted. "Emma, if we don't stop this now, they'll destroy everything. I can't let that happen."

"And I can't let you die," Emma shot back. "We figure this out together. No one gets left behind."

Lucas stared at her for a long moment, then nodded. "Together."

The Plan

Lucas examined the relay more closely, his mind racing. The structure was complex, its tendrils weaving into the rock like veins. Overloading it would take precision—and power.

"I can redirect the energy," he said finally. "Force it back into the core. But it'll take everything I have."

Emma frowned. "What does that mean? 'Everything you have'?"

Lucas hesitated. "It means I might not be able to maintain my form afterward. My energy reserves are already low."

Emma's stomach twisted. "So you'll... what? Fade away?"

"No," Lucas said quickly. "I'll recover. But it'll take time."

Emma nodded, though the knot in her chest didn't loosen. "What do you need me to do?"

Lucas glanced around the chamber. "Find anything you can to block the tunnel behind us. We need to slow them down if they break through the entrance."

Emma didn't argue. She moved quickly, gathering loose rocks and debris to pile at the tunnel's mouth. It wasn't much, but it would have to do.

Overload

Lucas stood before the relay, his glowing form flickering as he prepared to channel his energy. The structure pulsed in response, its tendrils writhing faintly as if sensing his intent.

"Emma," he said, his voice steady. "Whatever happens, stay back."

Emma swallowed hard, her throat tight. "Be careful."

Lucas nodded, then placed his hands on the relay. The room filled with a blinding light as his energy surged into the structure. The tendrils glowed brighter, their movements growing frantic as the core began to overload.

The ground trembled, cracks spreading across the chamber walls. Rocks tumbled from the ceiling, and the hum of the relay grew deafening.

"Lucas!" Emma shouted, shielding her face as the light intensified.

"I've got it!" Lucas yelled back, his voice strained. "Just a little longer!"

The relay's core fractured, its glowing tendrils snapping like overextended wires. The entire structure shuddered, its light flickering wildly.

"Get back!" Lucas shouted.

Emma stumbled toward the tunnel, her heart racing as the chamber began to collapse. She turned back just in time to see Lucas's form flicker one last time before the relay exploded in a burst of light and sound.

Aftermath

When the dust settled, Emma lay on the ground, her ears ringing and her body aching. The chamber was gone, reduced to rubble. Only faint traces of the relay's light remained, flickering weakly in the debris.

"Lucas?" she called, her voice hoarse.

A faint glow caught her eye, and she scrambled toward it. There, buried beneath the rubble, was Lucas. His form was dim, his energy flickering weakly, but he was alive.

"Emma," he said softly, his voice barely audible.

She knelt beside him, her eyes brimming with tears. "You did it. The relay's gone."

Lucas managed a faint smile. "For now."

CHAPTER FOURTEEN

Emerging Shadows

The air in the cave was thick with dust and the faint glow of fading energy. Emma knelt beside Lucas, her hands trembling as she reached out to steady him. His glowing form flickered weakly, his usual strength reduced to a faint pulse.

"You're going to be okay," Emma said, her voice more desperate than confident.

Lucas gave her a faint smile, though it was strained. "I'll recover. But we need to move."

Emma glanced around the chamber. The relay was completely destroyed, its tendrils shattered and lifeless, but the cave was unstable. Small rocks tumbled from the ceiling, and a deep groaning sound echoed through the space.

"We don't have much time," Lucas said, his voice hoarse. "This place is coming down."

Emma slipped her arm under his, helping him to his feet. He winced but didn't protest as they began moving toward the tunnel. The floor beneath them trembled with each step, and Emma's heart pounded with the fear that they wouldn't make it out in time.

The Narrow Escape

The tunnel they had entered through was blocked by debris, but Lucas guided Emma toward another passage. His glowing eyes flickered as he scanned the cave, his senses attuned to the faint vibrations of the earth.

"This way," he said, nodding toward a narrow crevice.

Emma hesitated. "Are you sure? That looks... tight."

"It's the only way," Lucas replied, his tone firm.

She swallowed hard and helped him through the crevice, the walls scraping against their shoulders as they squeezed through. The sound of falling rocks grew louder behind them, and Emma fought the urge to panic.

After what felt like an eternity, they emerged into a smaller chamber. A faint breeze brushed against Emma's face, carrying with it the scent of fresh air.

"We're close," Lucas said, his voice faint but determined.

Back Into the Open

The cave opened up into a forested ravine, the morning sunlight cutting through the trees in golden beams. Emma collapsed onto the ground, gasping for air as Lucas leaned heavily against a nearby boulder.

"We made it," she said, her voice filled with relief.

Lucas nodded, his glowing eyes scanning the area. "For now."

Emma frowned. "You always say that. Can't we take a second to breathe?"

Lucas didn't respond immediately. Instead, he straightened, his energy stabilizing as he began to recover. "The hunters know we're alive. They'll come for us."

Emma groaned, running a hand through her hair. "Do they ever take a day off?"

"Not until their mission is complete," Lucas said grimly. "And their mission is to eliminate me."

Emma looked at him, her expression hardening. "Then we make sure their mission fails."

The Hunters' Plan

Deep in the forest, the surviving hunters gathered in a concealed clearing. Their leader stood at the center, its glowing eyes narrowing as it surveyed the group. They were fewer in number now, their resources depleted, but their resolve was unshaken.

"The relay is gone," one of the hunters growled. "Zarneth is more dangerous than we anticipated."

The leader's lips curled into a snarl. "Dangerous, but weakened. He's vulnerable now."

"What about the human?" another asked. "She's helping him."

"She's irrelevant," the leader replied. "Zarneth is the target. Without him, this world is defenseless."

The hunters fell silent, their angular forms flickering faintly as they awaited the leader's command. Finally, the leader spoke, its voice cold and decisive.

"We strike tonight. No more waiting. No more games."

The others nodded, their movements sharp and precise. The hunt was far from over.

Preparing for the Final Battle

Back in Evergreen, Lucas and Emma returned to his house under the cover of dusk. The streets were quiet, the town blissfully unaware of the danger lurking nearby. Lucas sank onto the couch, his energy still low but slowly recovering. Emma paced the room, her mind racing.

"They're going to come for us," she said, her voice tight. "We can't just sit here and wait."

"We won't," Lucas replied. "But we need a plan."

Emma stopped, her eyes narrowing. "We need help."

Lucas shook his head. "No. The more people involved, the more dangerous it becomes. The hunters will target anyone who gets in their way."

Emma clenched her fists. "So what? We just do this alone?"

Lucas met her gaze, his expression serious. "We have no choice."

Emma sighed, her frustration bubbling over. "There has to be something we can do to even the odds."

Lucas hesitated, then stood. "There is one thing."

Emma's brow furrowed. "What?"

Lucas moved to a small hidden compartment in the floor, revealing a device she had never seen before. It was sleek and metallic, its surface glowing faintly with alien symbols.

"This is a disruptor," Lucas explained. "It's a last resort. If activated, it will release a pulse that disables all energy-based lifeforms within a certain radius."

Emma's eyes widened. "Including you?"

Lucas nodded. "Including me."

Emma stared at him, her chest tightening. "You're serious."

"It's the only way to ensure the hunters are eliminated," Lucas said. "But it's risky. If we're too close when it goes off..."

Emma's stomach twisted. "No. There has to be another way."

Lucas placed a hand on her shoulder, his touch surprisingly gentle. "Emma, we're out of time. If we don't stop them now, they'll destroy everything."

Emma looked at him, her resolve hardening. "Then we make sure it works. And we both walk away."

Lucas nodded, though his eyes betrayed his doubt. "Together."

The Calm Before the Storm

As night fell, Lucas and Emma prepared for the final confrontation. The disruptor sat on the table between them, its faint glow casting eerie shadows across the room. Outside, the streets of Evergreen were silent, the town blissfully unaware of the battle about to unfold.

Emma glanced at Lucas, her heart heavy. "If this works... what happens to you?"

Lucas hesitated. "I don't know."

Emma swallowed hard, her chest tightening. "Then we make sure it doesn't come to that."

Lucas gave her a faint smile. "You've always been stubborn."

She smirked, though it didn't reach her eyes. "You're just figuring that out now?"

They sat in silence for a moment, the weight of the coming battle pressing down on them. Finally, Lucas stood, his glowing form steady.

"It's time."

Closing of the Novel: "Beneath Our Skies"

CHAPTER FIFTEEN

The Final Stand

Lucas and Emma stood together in the empty streets of Evergreen, the disruptor clutched tightly in Lucas's hand. The town was eerily quiet, the calm before the storm. The hunters were coming, and they both knew there was no turning back.

As the first shadowy figures emerged from the forest, Lucas stepped forward, his glowing form illuminating the darkness. He turned to Emma one last time.

"Whatever happens, remember—this fight is bigger than me. Protect the town. Protect yourself."

Emma's eyes glistened with unshed tears, but she nodded, her voice steady. "We do this together."

The battle erupted in a flurry of light and energy. The hunters advanced relentlessly, their glowing eyes filled with malice, but Lucas met them head-on, his power blazing brighter than Emma had ever seen. Every strike was precise, every movement a testament to his strength and determination.

But it wasn't enough.

The hunters overwhelmed him, their numbers and ferocity pushing him to the brink. Emma watched in horror, her heart pounding as she realized what he was about to do.

Lucas activated the disruptor.

A blinding pulse of light surged outward, engulfing everything in its path. The hunters disintegrated instantly, their forms dissolving into the ether. The energy consumed the street, the trees, and Lucas himself.

Emma screamed his name, running toward him as the light faded. When the dust settled, the hunters were gone, and the disruptor lay silent in the street.

But Lucas was nowhere to be found.

Epilogue: Beneath Our Skies

Weeks passed, and Evergreen began to heal. The strange events were chalked up to rumors, stories that no one could prove. The townspeople moved on, unaware of the hero who had saved them.

Emma, however, couldn't forget. She walked the streets at night, hoping for a sign, a flicker of light, anything to indicate that Lucas was still out there. But the silence was deafening.

One evening, as she sat on the porch of her home, staring up at the stars, a faint shimmer caught her eye. A glow, fleeting but unmistakable, danced across the horizon.

A smile broke across her face, and her heart swelled with hope.

"Beneath our skies," she whispered, "you're still here."

The end wasn't final. It was a beginning—a promise that somewhere, Lucas was watching, protecting, and waiting for the world to be ready to know the truth.

Extended Closing: Chapter 15 - The Final Stand (Continued)

The disruptor's pulse rippled through the forest like a tidal wave of light, silencing everything in its path. Emma shielded her face with her arm as the sheer force of the energy left the air trembling. When it finally subsided, the street was quiet—eerily so. The hunters, once a relentless threat, were no more.

Emma blinked through the haze of dust and light, her chest tightening. "Lucas?" she called out, her voice raw.

Her steps faltered as she moved through the rubble, scanning for the faint glow of his energy. The disruptor lay inert on the ground, its metallic surface darkened. But Lucas... Lucas was gone.

"No," Emma whispered, panic rising in her chest. "No, no, no."

She dropped to her knees, her hands clutching at the dirt. Her mind raced, replaying every moment of the battle, every word Lucas had spoken. She refused to believe it had ended like this.

Epilogue: A Spark in the Dark

The days after the battle were filled with questions, but Emma offered no answers. The townspeople speculated about the strange light in the forest and the brief power surge that followed, but there was no evidence to confirm their suspicions. To them, it was a mystery, one they were content to let fade into obscurity.

But for Emma, the loss lingered. She spent her nights gazing at the sky, the stars a silent reminder of the man who had saved them all. She couldn't shake the feeling that he was still out there, somewhere, waiting.

Months Later

A cold wind blew through Evergreen as Emma walked the familiar path through the woods. The forest had begun to heal, the scars of the hunters' presence slowly fading. But Emma's own wounds remained fresh, the memory of Lucas's sacrifice haunting her every step.

She paused by a small clearing, the same place where Lucas had first revealed his true form to her. The air felt different here—charged, alive. Emma closed her eyes, letting the sensation wash over her.

And then, she felt it.

A faint hum, so soft it was almost imperceptible. Her eyes flew open, scanning the shadows. At first, there was nothing. Then, a faint shimmer—a ripple in the air that sent her heart racing.

"Lucas?" she whispered, her voice trembling.

The shimmer grew brighter, coalescing into a soft, golden light. Slowly, a familiar figure emerged, his form flickering as though caught between worlds. Lucas stood before her, his glowing eyes meeting hers.

"Emma," he said, his voice steady but laced with weariness.

Tears filled her eyes as she took a shaky step forward. "You're alive?"

"Barely," Lucas admitted, his form stabilizing. "The disruptor drained almost everything I had. It took... time to recover."

Emma didn't hesitate. She threw her arms around him, her relief overwhelming. "You came back."

Lucas returned the embrace, his energy warm and steady. "I never left."

A New Beginning

In the weeks that followed, Lucas remained a shadow in Evergreen, a protector unseen by most but known to Emma. They spoke often, planning for the future, preparing for the possibility that the hunters' remnants might someday return.

"You don't have to do this alone anymore," Emma told him one evening as they stood beneath the stars. "We're a team."

Lucas smiled faintly, his golden eyes reflecting the starlight. "A team."

As they stood together, the stars seemed to shine brighter, a silent promise of hope and resilience. The fight wasn't over, but neither were they.

And somewhere, beneath those same skies, the world carried on—unaware of the alien and the human who had fought to protect it, together.

FROM PCOD TO MOTHERHOOD: JOURNEY OF FAITH & FERTILITY

GEETA N. KHANDARE